THE MAGIC OF KINDNESS

Heddy Clark

On the first day of October, the spookiest month of the year, Victor found a basket of kittens on the doorstep of the Cat Witch Academy.
"They probably didn't know that the Academy only teaches witchcraft to cats that are at least six months old," said Headmistress Evie.

Evie gave the kittens some mashed pumpkin. "I hope Alice, the evil witch, doesn't find out they're here. From October 1st 'til Halloween, she casts evil spells on every kitten she finds."

"MEOW, MEOW, MEOW," cried the kittens.
Uh, oh, thought the headmistress.
"Evie!" called Victor. "I hear Alice flying outside." Just then, there was a LOUD knock on the door.

"Hurry, hide the kittens," cried Evie. "I'll get the door!"
With a wave of his wand, Victor turned the kittens into bats.

Alice flew past Evie. "Where are they? I know you have kittens!"
"Kittens?" said Evie as she swooshed her tail. "We don't accept kittens in the Academy."

"MEEOOOWWWW," howled the kittens.

"I knew it," snapped Alice. With a zap from her wand, she switched the bats back into kittens. Cackling, she swooped them up. "They're mine now!" In a puff of smoke, she and the kittens disappeared.

"We've got to save them!" said Evie, pacing the room. "I've got it! We'll sneak into Alice's lair and take the kittens back." The dreadful witch would fly about every night, so they waited 'til the sun went down to set off on their mission.

"I-It's d-dark in here," said Victor. Before Evie could say a word, four pairs of yellow, glowing eyes glared at them. Sharp fangs jutted from the kittens' mouths, and their knife-like claws slashed through the air.

"YOWL!" cried Victor. He hopped on his broom and zoomed out of the lair with Evie right behind. "It's too late." Victor said. "The kittens are cursed."

"No," said Evie. "I've got an idea. We'll find Alice's spell book and reverse the spell."

The next day, the good witches woke extra early and flew to Alice's lair. Careful not to wake Alice, they looked in every closet and chest, even under Alice's bed. "It has to be here," whispered Evie as she stumbled into a metal suit of armor.

Suddenly, the wall moved. Behind it was a hidden library. Thousands of books towered above them.

"How will we find it?" asked Victor.
"We'll use witch-charm!" Evie pointed her wand in the air. "Show us the book with the secret spell that turns mean spirits to kind."
"Look," whispered Victor. "That one's glowing."

With a quick leap and a swipe of her paw, Evie got the book.
"Now, back to the Academy," said Victor.

Inside the book, written in blood, Evie found what she was looking for. It read:

A friendly and generous offering of some tasty stew will likely change wicked witches and cats from evil to good.

Snake skins
Goblin wings
Toad warts
Beetle eggs
Honey

The two witches went to work. In a cauldron, they brewed snake skins, goblin wings, toad warts, and beetle eggs. Almost done, they added a dab of honey for taste.

"Purr-fect," said Evie. They dashed back to Alice's lair and offered the stew to the kittens. Soon, their hisses and growls turned to sweet little purrs. "They're back!" said Victor.

As the cats were leaving, Alice stormed in. "Who dares to come into my lair?" Evie's tail puffed up twice its size and Victor shook. "I-I thought you might like a delicious meal," said Evie.

Alice pointed her skinny, crooked finger at the cats. "You're lucky I'm hungry, but do this again and I'll turn you into slugs!"

Alice gobbled up every last bite. "Now get out of here. I have more scaring to do." But as she licked the bottom of her bowl, Alice tripped over her broom.

THUD! "Are you okay?" asked Evie.
"I can't move my leg! I think it's broken." Alice tried to get up but fell back down.

Evie and Victor used their magic dust to ease Alice's pain. "We'll help you 'til your leg heals," said Evie. "All the cat witches at the Academy will be happy to help."

"No one's ever been nice to me before," cooed Alice. Evie looked past Alice to the kittens. "Oh yes," said Alice. "Take your kittens. I only made them evil so I could have some company."

"I've got it," said Evie. "What if you help us at the Academy? You'll have lots of company!"

Alice smiled. "I'd love that."

Moving close to Evie. Victor whispered. "The spell worked."
Evie thought for a moment. then asked. "Was it the spell or the kindness we showed?"

"You know," Evie said as she tapped her chin, "I think I'll send a memo out tomorrow. This kindness thing is powerful magic."

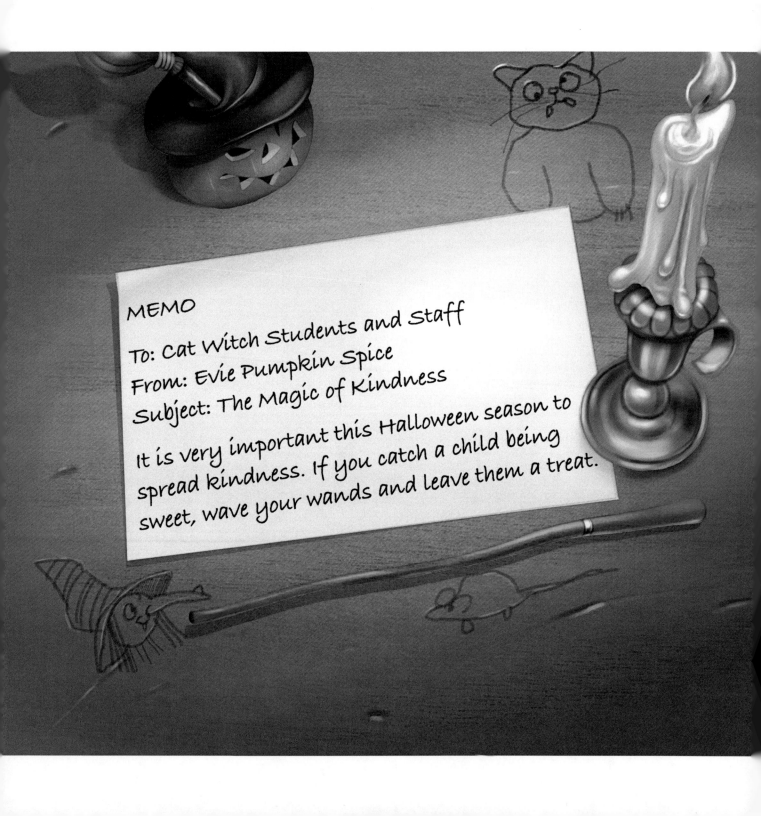

MEMO

To: Cat Witch Students and Staff
From: Evie Pumpkin Spice
Subject: The Magic of Kindness

It is very important this Halloween season to spread kindness. If you catch a child being sweet, wave your wands and leave them a treat.

Affectionately dedicated to my mother and father, who taught me the magic of kindness and hard work.

THE MAGIC OF KINDNESS
© Heddy Clark, 2022

For information about permission to reproduce selections from this book, contact HeddyClark.com

First printed in 2022 in the United States of America.

Please visit HeddyClark.com for more information.

This book was designed, laid out, proofread, and publicized by an Editwright team.
Visit editwright.com for more Editwright works.

Editing by Andrew Doty
Book design by Andrea Reider
Illustrations by Leo Brown
Proofreading by Dana Zwaska

Published by Hockett Drake Publishing

Hardcover: 979-8-9850965-0-7
Paperback: 979-8-9850965-1-4
E-book: 979-8-9850965-2-1

Library of Congress Control Number: 2021925285

Library of Congress Cataloguing-in-Publication Data available upon request.

Special thanks to Andrew Doty at Editwright for helping to make this book a reality.